Clark Kent & lab partner—
future scientists!

DC COMICS
SECRET HERO SOCIETY

SCIENCE FAIR CRISIS

Written by **Derek Fridolfs** | Illustrations by **Pamela Lovas** and **Shane Clester**

SCHOLASTIC INC.

To my parents, who helped me with my own science fair project. And for Pamela, who has joined me on many projects since.

— Derek

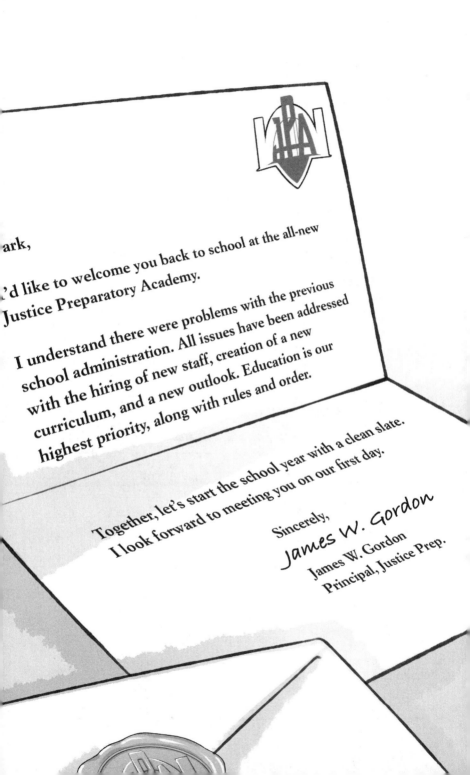

ark,

'd like to welcome you back to school at the all-new
Justice Preparatory Academy.

I understand there were problems with the previous
school administration. All issues have been addressed
with the hiring of new staff, creation of a new
curriculum, and a new outlook. Education is our
highest priority, along with rules and order.

Together, let's start the school year with a clean slate.
I look forward to meeting you on our first day.

Sincerely,

James W. Gordon

James W. Gordon
Principal, Justice Prep.

8

9

⭐ S.T.A.R.

S.T.A.R. LABS
"Tomorrow's Technology Today"

The Scientific and Technological Advanced Research Labs have been responsible for many of the greatest scientific achievements in the world, including our latest invention . . . the construction of an experimental teleportation beam, to explore our vast solar system.

Now we are looking toward the future by helping to fos the minds of tomorrow! Thi brochure will help provide you with helpful tips for entr into your school's science fa competition.

SCIENCE FAIR—
STUDENT GUIDELINES

- Projects should be the work of the individual student.

- Research the materials of your subject.

- Experiments should be safe and not harm others.

- You will be judged on originality, presentation, and creativity.

- Remember to have fun!!!

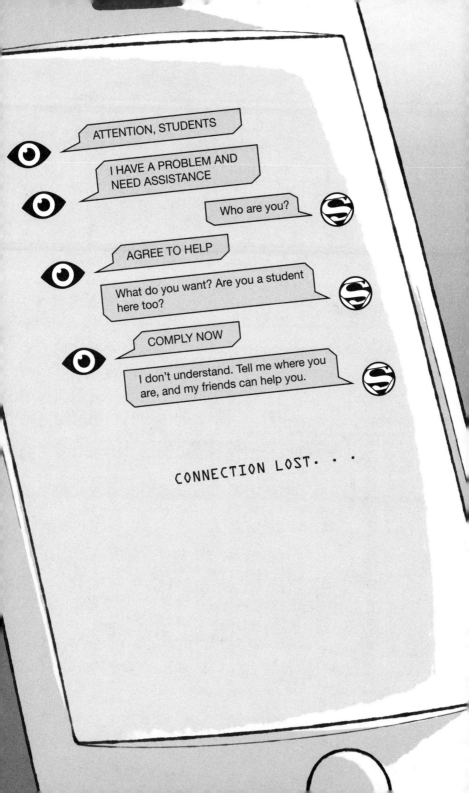

JUSTICE PREP—STUDENT COMPUTER LAB
STUDENT LOG-IN = VIC_STONE
USER PASSWORD = *****
ACCESS GRANTED

ORACLE SEARCH ENGINE
ENTER SEARCH QUERY . . .

FIND USER = <EYE>

TRACKING SOURCE . . .

SOURCE NUMBER = UNLISTED
IP ADDRESS = LOCATION UNKNOWN

TO: JUSTICESQUAD
FROM: VIC_STONE
RE: MYSTERY EYE

I'VE BEEN UNSUCCESSFUL IN FINDING OUT
ANYTHING ABOUT OUR "MYSTERY EYE." THE SCHOOL
SOFTWARE'S PROXY DETECTOR HAS BEEN UNABLE
TO LOCATE THE SERVER USED OR TRIANGULATE
ANY CELL PHONE TOWERS TO PINPOINT WHERE THE
TRANSMISSION CAME FROM. EVEN THOUGH WE ALL
GOT THE SAME TEXTS TO OUR PHONES, IT'S LIKE
THE SOURCE OF THE MESSAGE DOESN'T EVEN EXIST!

TO: IN~~JUSTICE PREP~~ CLUB

LOOKING TO JOIN THE COOL KIDS?

BRING YOUR BAD SELF TO OUR BASEMENT RETREAT. FOOD AND FUN PROVIDED (WE'LL JUST BREAK INTO THE VENDING MACHINES).

LET'S HAVE FUN PLOTTING OUR NEXT MISSION TO TAKE OVER THE WORLD.

BWAH HAH HAH HAH HAH HAH HAH HAH HAH HAH HAH HAH HAH HAH!!!

Hey, Clark. Found this note being passed around the school. Looks like we're not the only ones trying to meet up. Not so paranoid now, am I? Tell Barry that.

— Bruce

September 5th

CLARK'S JOURNAL

It's great to be back at school and see all my friends again! Ducard Academy has been renamed Justice Preparatory Academy. And hopefully the name isn't the only thing that's changed.

The new principal seems eager to keep everyone in line and focus on education. He seems pretty no-nonsense, and I bet he'd make a good police officer. We've got new ID cards and new teachers. And a school science fair to take part in. So I think things are looking up.

But Bruce still believes there's always danger around every corner. I don't always believe that, but then he showed me that note, and he snuck in on a secret meeting with a lot of the school bullies. So maybe there is something sinister lurking in the shadows.

And then there's the Mystery Eye itself. Everyone in school, even the bullies, seems to have gotten the strange text messages from it. We have no idea who it is or what they want. So I guess this new mystery will keep us busy trying to get to the bottom of it.

Dr. Alec Holland
Science

Professor Martin Stein
Physics

Professor Eobard Thawne
Science

Mr. John Henry Irons
Shop Class

Professor Rudolph Jones
Math

Mr. Lawrence Crock
PE/Swim Coach

SCIENCE CLASSROOM SYLLABUS

Teacher: Dr. Alec Holland
Class: Room 92

Students will learn about various science topics and how they are relevant to their lives. Students are encouraged to explore topics through discussion, debate, and writing. Topics of study will include Earth history, cells, genetics, life science, and the physiology of plants and animals.

Students will identify the Earth's major biomes, be able to classify organisms, and examine the characteristics and properties of matter. In the process, they will develop critical thinking skills to solve problems.

I only require everyone to be respectful of our Earth and each other, be responsible, and be safe. I hope by learning about the world around you, it will help inspire your science fair projects!

PROFESSOR **EOBARD THAWNE'S**

"SCIENCE AT THE SPEED OF LIGHT"

ZOOOOOOOOOM ZOOOOOOOOOM

TAKING KNOWLEDGE FROM THE PAST, PRESENT, AND FUTURE, MY COURSE IS DESIGNED TO STUDY HOW SCIENCE CAN HELP CHANGE OUR LIVES.

- IDENTIFY NEWTON'S THREE LAWS OF MOTION AND APPLY THEM TO DISTANCE, SPEED, VELOCITY, AND TIME.
- BECOME FAMILIAR WITH THE FORMS AND TRANSFORMATIONS OF ENERGY.
- STUDY THE RELATIONSHIP BETWEEN FORCE, MASS, AND MOTION OF OBJECTS.
- EXAMINE THE CHARACTERISTICS OF GRAVITY, ELECTRICITY, AND MAGNETISM.

DON'T BE LATE!
DON'T FALL BEHIND!
DON'T BE SLOW TURNING IN YOUR ASSIGNMENTS!

INTRODUCTION TO PHYSICS

Instructor: Professor Martin Stein

I will promote the discovery process within physics, and Earth and space sciences. Students will carry out experiments that will allow them to discover physical principles using lab skills and math. We will also discuss the connections between physical science principles, current technologies, and their impact on society.

The following topics will be covered, including:

- The study of mass, volume, area, temperature, and acceleration.

- Calculating the gravitational effects between two bodies.

- Discussing the solar system and the laws of motion in relation to the planets.

- Demonstrating the conservation and transformation of energy.

- The relationships between temperature, heat, and thermal energy.

- Discussing other forms of electromagnetic radiation.

- Discovering the relationships between magnetism and electricity.

I will be happy to help guide you in determining your science fair project, and will make myself available during and after school.

MATH CLASS SYLLABUS
Professor Rudolph Jones
Room P8

This course is designed to prepare students for algebra and geometry. Through a sequence of mathematical topics, students will pick up skills, learn from those around them, and extend their knowledge of math to promote confidence and mastery.

I will cover the following: numbers and operations, calculator applications, solving equations, graphing, transformations, parallel lines, theorems, volume and surface area, and many other topics.

As a former employee of S.T.A.R. Labs, I know what their review staff is looking for when judging the science fair. I'm ready to share my knowledge with you, if you're willing to share your projects with me.

Be prepared to absorb as much information as possible.

JOHN HENRY IRONS
SHOP CLASS 101

My class will cover metal and wood shop, and the basic skills in using hand and power tools in an industrial environment. We'll go over tool use, equipment know-how, selecting materials, measuring, bench works, basic mechanical drawings, environmental awareness, and preventive maintenance.

You must wear protective goggles, gloves, and the correct clothing in order to work in class. It's extremely important to follow all instructions, proper procedures, and safety measures.

NO HORSEPLAY ALLOWED!

I can help guide you in the assembly and construction of your science fair project, in class or during lunch break. Sign in at the front desk to inquire about times to use any tools under my supervision.

SWIM TEAM TRYOUTS

Think you can master the sport of swimming?

Let's see what you got!

≈ **Learn and improve techniques on the four swim strokes**
   (freestyle, backstroke, breaststroke, butterfly)

≈ **Boost self-confidence!**

≈ **Compete against the best!**

≈ **Swim to win!**

To register, contact Coach Crusher
Lawrence Crock / PE and Swim Team Coach

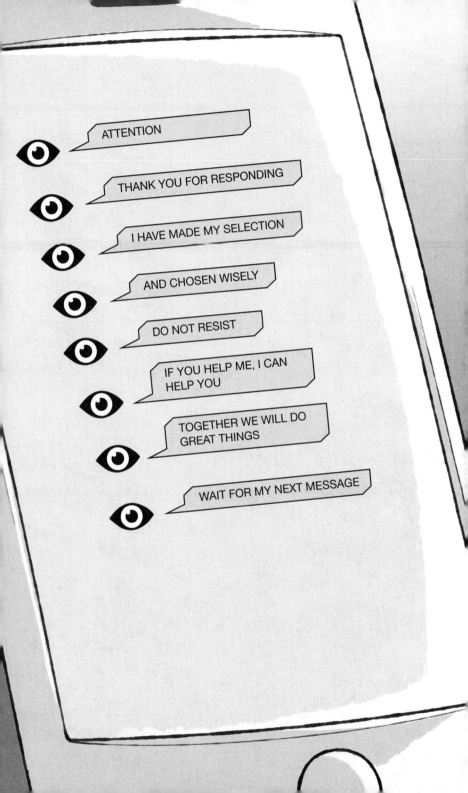

CLARK'S JOURNAL

Compared to Ducard Academy, I'm really liking all my new teachers here at Justice Prep.

Science class with Dr. Holland is going to be fun. He's really encouraging us to become close to nature and open our eyes to the bigger, greener world out there. Professor Stein's physics class almost seems like an accident waiting to happen. But I don't know if that's because of all the fire extinguishers in class or because the Joker is in there with us. Luckily I have Bruce as a lab partner to keep an eye on him. Math should be interesting since Professor Jones worked at S.T.A.R. Labs. I wonder why he's no longer there? But maybe he'll know how to help us with our science fair projects anyway. And shop class is great. It's a chance to be creative, as long as we follow the safety rules set by Mr. Irons.

Also, Arthur takes to water like a fish. He's already made the swim team, and continues to do better against the other kids in class.

But this Mystery Eye is still sending messages. The latest text sounds like he or she has found someone to accept the offer. So now the mystery has gotten bigger. Who is this Eye? And who is working with them? And for what purpose?

GOT THE SCOOP?

The school newspaper is looking for any information leading to the discovery of who is sending these mystery texts. Send in your information anonymously in our web forum, or come to our office and report it directly.

THE JUSTICE TRIBUNE

"Reporting the news...Reporting the truth"

THANK YOU!

40

41

JUSTICE PREP

JUSTICE PREP SCIENCE FAIR—SUBMISSION FORM

I am a proud science fair participant!

Student Name: Clark Kent

Teacher / Sponsor: Professor Martin Stein

Project Subject: something involving space and planets

Special instructions / setup:

I will need a table for my three-panel display board and any model or diorama sample I end up using.

Thank you.

48

What is "life science"? Any field of science that has the potential to lead to an enhanced understanding of living organisms.

- Two factors of ecosystems are biotic factors and abiotic factors.
- Biotic factors are any living thing in an ecosystem. These can include plants (trees, flowers, vegetation), bacteria (small organisms), and animals.
- Abiotic factors are nonliving things in an ecosystem. These can include sunlight, water, air, temperature, climate, and even rocks.

So what encompasses a whole ecosystem?

- It starts with the organism or life-form.
- Its niche is the role the organism plays.
- Its habitat is where it lives.
- Its population is how many are living there.
- Its community is what other things live alongside it.
- And ultimately, its ecosystem is both its biotic and abiotic factors, which balance life.

Hopefully our study of life science will give you a greater understanding of the world around you, what part each of us plays in it, and also might help inspire some ideas for your science fair projects!

50

I'm sure you all think math is all about numbers and is boring. Maybe you're right. But maybe it's more than that. So let's just skip the numbers part and talk about how the basics of math can help us solve problems.

READ the problem. What is the question to be answered?

THINK about what facts are given. Circle the facts needed to solve the problem.

SOLVE the problem. Look for patterns. Guess and check from your list to find it.

JUSTIFY the answer. What did you do? Why did you do it?

As a former employee at **S.T.A.R. Labs**, I know these are the things the judges will be looking for when evaluating your science fair projects. But always remember ...

If you can't come up with your own idea, then borrow one from someone else. But just ask first!

Okay, in all seriousness, math is about solving problems. And sometimes you need all the help you can get. So talk with others to find solutions, get ideas, share, and sometimes even take. The more you gain from others around you, the stronger you'll be.

52

SWIM TEAM— FINAL EXAM
Coach Crusher

ATTENTION, ATHLETES!

The time to race your fellow classmates is NOW! I want the best of the best. Be prepared to use any style necessary to achieve this goal. The winner of my exam will be awarded the highest position of team captain.

A team captain lives to swim. They must be fast and strong. They command respect. And they lead others to victory.

Swimmers MUST:
- ≈ Report to the pool at 2 p.m.
- ≈ Take part in mandatory warm-ups at 2:15.
- ≈ Be on time. Tardiness will remove you from the lineup and you will fail the exam.
- ≈ If you do, your device will be taken away and you will swim laps alone.
- ≈ Stay hydrated. Candy and soda are discouraged.
- ≈ Stay in team area AT ALL TIMES.
- ≈ Swim in ALL the events for the exam.

Will you lead my team as its captain? Okay, you pool rats, it's time to find out!

54

JOHN HENRY IRONS
SHOP CLASS 101

If you think it, you can build it!

Anything you're able to think up for the science fair, we can find a way to build it in this class. There's plenty of tools, equipment, and steelworks we can use to create your project.

You always wanted to build a volcano? Let's do it. You don't need to stick with just papier-mâché and baking soda and vinegar. Expand your mind. We can construct it out of wood, plaster, or metal. The component can be powered by gears or a battery. Anything is possible!

Why stick to the standard potato clock to produce electricity? Use your imagination. Maybe you want a super-toaster instead. We'll find a way to take it apart, observe the mechanics, fix any broken pieces, and rebuild it to your new blueprint specs.

If needed, I could even help you build a steel suit out of metal.

Safety is our utmost concern, so I will always be here to monitor and provide direction. But let's help your idea become a reality!

THE VELOCITY OF TIME

BY PROFESSOR EOBARD THAWNE

VELOCITY IS THE RATE OF CHANGE IN POSITION WITH RESPECT TO TIME. THIS INCLUDES BOTH THE MAGNITUDE AND DIRECTION. GOT THAT, BARRY?

THE AVERAGE VELOCITY IS WHAT A BODY EXPERIENCES OVER A GIVEN AMOUNT OF TIME. IT CAN BE FOUND BY DIVIDING THE TOTAL CHANGE IN DISPLACEMENT BY THE TOTAL TIME ELAPSED DURING THAT DISPLACEMENT. HOW IS THAT SO FAR, BARRY?

AVERAGE VELOCITY DOESN'T DESCRIBE EVERYTHING THAT HAPPENS DURING THE TIME INTERVAL. BUT YOU HAVE ABOVE-AVERAGE VELOCITY, BARRY. ALMOST INSTANTANEOUS. AND INSTANTANEOUS VELOCITY IS AN OBJECT AT ANY GIVEN INSTANT IN TIME.

KINETIC ENERGY OF A PARTICLE DEPENDS ON ITS MASS AND ITS VELOCITY. THE MOTION CAN BE EITHER TRANSLATIONAL, ROTATIONAL, OR VIBRATIONAL. OR ALL THREE FOR YOU, RIGHT, BARRY?

AND SPEED IS THE MAGNITUDE OF VELOCITY WITHOUT DIRECTION. BUT YOU ALREADY KNOW THAT, BARRY, BECAUSE YOU'RE FAST!!!

IN SUMMARY:

- POSITIVE VELOCITY IS MOVING FORWARD.
- NEGATIVE VELOCITY IS MOVING BACKWARD.
- ZERO VELOCITY IS STOPPED, MAYBE JUST FOR AN INSTANT.

WE'RE GOING TO NEED ALL OF THIS TO DO WHAT WE NEED TO DO NEXT, BARRY . . .

59

TO: Lois_Lane
FROM: Clark_Kent
SUBJECT: SCIENCE FAIR

Lois,

What's your project going to be for the science fair? I'm not trying to steal your idea. Just curious to have a rough idea. I'm still struggling to figure out what I want to do. Again, not that I want to steal your idea.

—CK

TO: Clark_Kent
FROM: Lois_Lane
SUBJECT: SCIENCE FAIR

RELAX, SMALLVILLE! YOU'RE NOT GOING TO STEAL
MY IDEA, BECAUSE I'M NOT ENTERING THE SCIENCE
FAIR THIS YEAR.

AS EDITOR AND REPORTER FOR THE NEWSPAPER,
I'VE TAKEN AN OATH TO REMAIN IMPARTIAL. IT'S
HARD TO GET SCOOPS AND WRITE ARTICLES TO DIG
UP THE TRUTH ABOUT IT IF I'M ACCUSED OF USING
MY POSITION TO GAIN SOME KIND OF ADVANTAGE.

BUT DON'T WORRY, FARM BOY. I'M NOT REQUIRING
YOU TO STEP DOWN OR ANYTHING. I'LL JUST
REMOVE YOU FROM WRITING ANY ARTICLES ABOUT
THE SCIENCE FAIR, OTHERWISE PEOPLE MIGHT
THINK I'M ENDORSING YOU. WELL . . . MAYBE . . .
WE'LL SEE.

JUST REMEMBER, IF YOU DO END UP WINNING THE
COMPETITION, THEN YOU OWE ME THE EXCLUSIVE
INTERVIEW.

UNTIL THEN, YOU JUST OWE ME LUNCH.

CLARK'S JOURNAL

As the science fair is getting closer, it's making me more nervous. Everyone else seems to be hard at work on their projects, some more secretive than others, but I haven't come up with the right idea for my own project. It doesn't help being distracted by who the Mystery Eye is.

I have found I'm enjoying working for the newspaper, though! Lois runs a tight ship over there. Always yelling and pointing where we should go, who to interview, and what to write. But it does keep things lively and exciting. I even think I have a knack for this, but it's too early to tell.

I better go. She's yelling at me to go proofread some articles before I make photocopies for the next edition. I might be faster than a locomotive, but sometimes I can barely keep up with her!

[MESSAGE DELETED]

is everyone here?

not Clark

that's a first

where is he?

wasting time

no he's working at the newspaper

that's cool

they write some great articles

I read it for the funnies

They don't print any comic strips Barry

WHAT?!

then who's drawing in my newspapers?

you probably were

yeah I get bored easy

any updates on the mystery eye

BOOOOOOORING

sorry for being late

hey Arthur

so check it

I've finished my science fair project

what is it?

come meet me in the library right now and I'll show you!

SEND

THE JUSTICE TRIBUNE

S.T.A.R. ATTRACTION
OUR INTERVIEW WITH THE SCIENTIST BEHIND THE SCIENCE

BY LOIS LANE

With the science fair quickly approaching, I thought we'd take the time to talk directly with the source of the science fair. I was able to get on the phone with the general director, Professor Emil Hamilton of S.T.A.R. Labs, to speak about the competition itself.

"We're always very excited to see what the students come up with each year. You'd be surprised, but it inspires us just to see them, as much as they might be inspired by visiting us here. Remember, they are all future scientists in the making!" gushed Professor Emil.

But what do they look for when it comes to judging?

"Students who ask great questions even if they don't have all the answers. Science is as much about the journey as the destination. Creativity goes a long way, as does unbridled enthusiasm. Because if you're excited to share your discovery, it can excite the world." And more importantly, the judges.

"I'm afraid I have to cut our interview short. I have to meet with one of my scientists about a recent discovery that fell into our lap, so to speak!"

And with that, our interview was over.

It sounds like there's a lot of things going on over at the labs in preparation for the science fair. And you should be just as busy here. Word has it that Arthur Curry's project is the one to beat for the top prize, having revealed it recently to his close friends. But don't let that stop you from getting your own projects done in the race to win. We're all cheering for you as you represent Justice Prep.

Go, future scientists!

MYSTERY EYE SUSPECTS

Bane = Bully but low on the totem pole. Does he even know how to text?

David Hyde = Swimmer. More interested in chlorine than computers.

Edward Nigma = Genius intellect. But it's not like him to not use riddles.

Harley Quinn = Along for the ride to have fun. Not a criminal mastermind.

The Joker = Unpredictable! Might do it for a laugh, or fool us into thinking it.

Lex Luthor = Always plotting something, even if he's no longer at our school.

Pamela Isley = More interested in plants than people. What's her motive?

Noah Kuttler = Always has his head in his calculator. Suspicious.

Johnny Corben = Always lurking around. Cutting corners. Easily aggravated.

Winslow Schott = Loves toys. But could the Mystery Eye be his greatest toy?

Lois Lane = Clark vouches for her, but I never trust the press. Watch her!

Dr. Alec Holland = Good teacher. Don't know much about him.

Professor Martin Stein = Overly cautious, which isn't a bad thing.

Mr. John Henry Irons = Works with his hands. Not sure if he'd be involved in this.

Professor Eobard Thawne = An unknown. Seems focused on one thing.

Professor Rudolph Jones = Former S.T.A.R. Labs employee. Need to check his history.

Principal James Gordon = The last principal turned out to be a villain. Might be again. We'll see.

Alfred = "The butler always does it" I hear. So I just had to be safe listing him. Sorry, Alfred. Please don't take away my desserts for the week.

LUTHORCORP—PRIVATE CHAT ROOM
USERS LOGGED IN = 2
[1 KNOWN, 1 GUEST]

Lex I've got a question for you. **C**

Why hello Clark.

What an unexpected surprise.

Were you responsible for the lab accident today? **C**

I have no idea what you're talking about.

I don't go to your school anymore, remember?

And why is it when something goes wrong, you assume I'm responsible?

Because you usually are. **C**

Just because I had my own lab accident that burned off my hair

doesn't mean I'm responsible for EVERY lab accident.

right **C**

But it's nice to know you care.

Now don't be a stranger. Drop by anytime.

[GUEST LOGGED OUT]

jerk

SEND

THE JUSTICE TRIBUNE

SEEDS OF SUSPICION
DISASTROUS OVERGROWTH IN SCIENCE LAB LEAVES STUDENTS SHAKEN AND TEACHER SICK

BY LOIS LANE

When you go to class, you expect a boring lecture, maybe a pop quiz, or to take an exam. You never expect the classroom to attack you! But that's just what happened in Dr. Alec Holland's science class yesterday.

A plant science experiment to show the process of photosynthesis took a drastic turn when the entire classroom came under attack. "It's like it turned into a swamp in here," offered one student. "One minute we were looking in our microscopes. The next, we were fighting off crazy vines and killer plants!"

Dr. Alec Holland, known for his admiration of green conservation and plant life, did not report to school today. He's out sick, possibly the result of an allergic reaction to pollen in his class.

"Dr. Holland is a brilliant teacher," claims Pamela Isley, one of his prize students. "He has a great love for the green. He'd never do something that would harm it or the rest of us."

With this being the second laboratory accident this past week, it's been noted tha both have possible ties to each other. Both had a liquid or chemical component resulted in the damage caused. But at this time, Dr. Holland has been ruled ou possible suspect.

CLARK'S JOURNAL

Bruce thought it would be a good idea to investigate the school at night. With all the classrooms being vandalized, I think he hoped we'd catch someone in the act. Instead, a monster almost caught us!

A weird package was sent to our math teacher's classroom, addressed to Rudy Jones. When Professor Jones opened it, it affected him. Bruce ran the box through his computer lab back home and found traces of radiation. The exposure must have transformed Mr. Jones into that monster. It was like a living parasite, because when it touched us, it started to absorb our powers. I think it might've absorbed the energy from some of the student experiments and destroyed the classroom. He would've gotten away with damaging more things, too, if it weren't for us kids showing up. Thankfully Diana's lasso caught him, calmed him until he reverted back to normal, and made him tell the truth. Professor Jones wasn't responsible.

The package had no return address, so there's no way to know where it came from. But I have my guesses who might've sent it . . . our Mystery Eye!

TO: Clark_Kent
FROM: Bruce_Wayne
SUBJECT: Shop Class Investigation

I managed to get to the room while it was undisturbed. No teacher or students were around. I was able to recover some evidence at the scene.

I ran the sample of water I took. It has ocean components to it. That's not a direct indication of who might've done this. But it points to a few suspects who might talk to fish.

Speaking of which, the dead fish I took as evidence didn't have a smile on it. None of them did. So unless he forgot to put lipstick on them, I don't think the Joker is responsible here.

I did a quick scan for footprints or fingerprints but came up empty.

One thing, though . . . the janitor has been seen at every room that's been damaged. It's his job to clean them, but is he the one responsible for destroying them? It's something to consider.

SEND

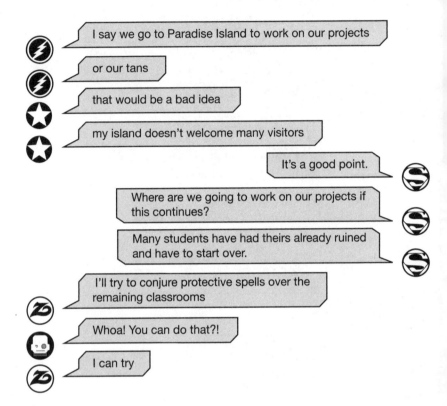

I say we go to Paradise Island to work on our projects

or our tans

that would be a bad idea

my island doesn't welcome many visitors

It's a good point.

Where are we going to work on our projects if this continues?

Many students have had theirs already ruined and have to start over.

I'll try to conjure protective spells over the remaining classrooms

Whoa! You can do that?!

I can try

SEND

Arthur are you there?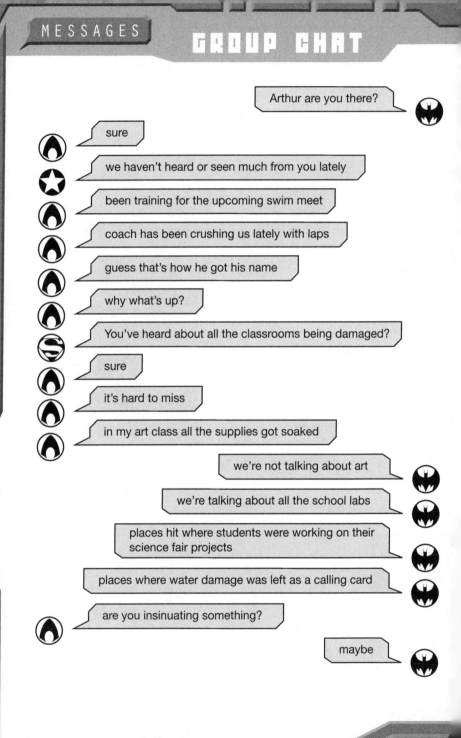

sure

we haven't heard or seen much from you lately

been training for the upcoming swim meet

coach has been crushing us lately with laps

guess that's how he got his name

why what's up?

You've heard about all the classrooms being damaged?

sure

it's hard to miss

in my art class all the supplies got soaked

we're not talking about art

we're talking about all the school labs

places hit where students were working on their science fair projects

places where water damage was left as a calling card

are you insinuating something?

maybe

SEND

THE JUSTICE TRIBUNE

CAUGHT WET-HANDED
MULTIPLE DAMAGED CLASSROOMS LINKED TO ONE GUILTY STUDENT

BY LOIS LANE

Sometimes all you need to do to find someone guilty is wait for them to wash up right under your nose. That's how Principal Gordon put this case to rest.

There have been multiple classroom labs vandalized and destroyed over the past few weeks. Science labs, the physics lab, shop class, and even the math class have all met their destruction. But it was the boys' restroom blowing up that solved this wet whodunit!

With Arthur Curry being the only person seen exiting the flooded restroom after it exploded, in front of the principal, it finally made sense. All of the damages have been water related.

Arthur of the swim team. Arthur, camp lifeguard. And now Arthur . . . former student at Justice Preparatory Academy?

Principal Gordon not only disqualified Arthur from entering his project into the upcoming science fair, but he also has sent him home. It's undetermined when or if he'll return to school.

"I'm not responsible! I swear!" shouted Arthur, before he was walked off the campus. But all soggy signs point to him.

GOOD MORNING, JUSTICE PREP!

THIS IS PRINCIPAL GORDON WITH YOUR DAILY REPORT.

I WOULD LIKE TO START BY DISCUSSING THE RECENT SUSPENSION OF STUDENT ARTHUR CURRY. AFTER HIS INVOLVEMENT IN SCHOOL VANDALISM, AND HIS DISQUALIFICATION FROM THE UPCOMING SCIENCE FAIR, THE SCHOOL BOARD HAS DECIDED TO SUSPEND HIM EFFECTIVE IMMEDIATELY. WHILE I WILL CONDUCT MY OWN FORMAL INVESTIGATION, I'D LIKE TO WARN THE STUDENT BODY THAT DISCIPLINARY ACTION WILL BE TAKEN ON ANYONE FOUND RESPONSIBLE FOR ANY WRONGDOING BEFORE THE SCIENCE FAIR.

ON A LIGHTER NOTE, DON'T FORGET THAT TOMORROW IS PICTURE DAY. COME DRESSED READY TO SMILE!

DUE TO ONGOING MAINTENANCE, DAMAGED ROOMS AND LABS WILL BE CLOSED UNTIL FURTHER NOTICE. NEW ROOM SCHEDULES AND LOCATIONS HAVE BEEN POSTED IN THE AUDITORIUM.

CLUBS MEETING TODAY INCLUDE THE COBBLEPOT AVIARY SOCIETY, SWIM CLUB, AND THE CHESS CLUB. CHECKMATE!

AS A REMINDER, ALL COOKIE FUND-RAISER MONEY SHOULD BE TURNED IN TO THE OFFICE TREASURY SECRETARY BEFORE THE END OF THE WEEK.

NEXT UP, WE HAVE THE WEATHER FORECAST BY STUDENT VICTOR FRIES . . .

THE JUSTICE TRIBUNE

EDITORIAL OPINION

PRESIDENTIAL PARDON ME?

BY JOHN CORBEN

Something stinks in this school, and it isn't just the fish sandwiches in the cafeteria. Ex–swim team athlete Arthur Curry has been kicked out of school due to all the damage he's caused. Were they silly pranks that got out of hand? Or was something more sinister behind his involvement? It's unknown at this point. But what is known are his ties to Clark Kent.

The two share a history dating back to Camp Evergreen, where Arthur was a lifeguard at the lake when Clark was enrolled there. The lake has its own history of missing kids and accidents that Arthur didn't prevent, most likely with help from Clark. And I'm sure Clark had a hand in convincing his friend to come to Justice Prep, so they could continue to plot ways to cause problems. There are even some whispers around campus of a secret club they're involved in, that I'm sure is up to no good.

You're only as good as the friends you keep. So I ask: should Clark Kent still be class president or write for this very newspaper with his friendship and involveme with suspended student Arthur Curry? I enthusiastically say NO!

Let your voices be heard, Justice Prep!

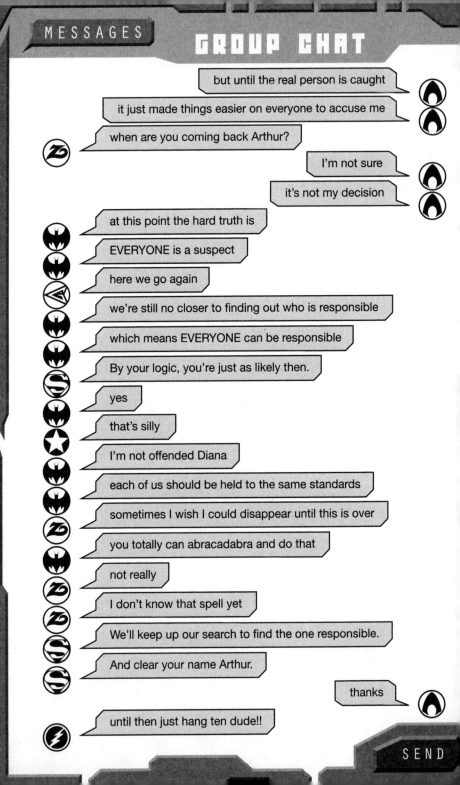

November 6th

CLARK'S JOURNAL

If there's anything I've found out, it's that school is never boring.

Johnny Corben wrote this weird article about me and Arthur. It's like he has some kind of grudge against me, but I don't know what I ever did to him. He writes lies and makes things up, which goes against what Lois and I are doing at the paper. We're trying to find the truth. And when he was confronted about what he wrote, he got mad and quit the newspaper. It's probably for the best. But I have a feeling it's not the last I'll hear from him.

With Arthur being disqualified from the science fair and suspended, it's got us all on edge. Everyone is looking over their shoulder and nervous about what will happen next or who will be accused of something. It's almost like we've all become as paranoid as Bruce is.

Who has time to work on their science fair project when someone is out to get them?

Clark, I was able to grab all these notes passed in class. Don't know if any of them will help find our suspect.   —Barry

If you give me water, I will die. What am I?
—E. Nigma

Answer: FIRE

I am a word. If you pronounce me right, it will be wrong. If you pronounce me wrong, it is right. What word am I? —E. Nigma

Answer: WRONG

I don't have eyes, ears, nose, or tongue, but I can see, smell, hear, and taste everything. What am I?   —E. Nigma

Answer: A BRAIN

I can see but can't hear or speak. But I will always tell the truth. What am I?

—E. Nigma

Answer: A MIRROR

Roses are red, violets are blue
If I catch you hurting flowers, that will be the end of you!

—Pamela

IT'S HARD TO WRITE SMALL WITH LARGE HANDS
—GIGANTA!

!!! EMERGENCY SPY-HACK ALERT !!!

ANTISPY SOFTWARE HAS DETECTED A DANGEROUS
HACK TO YOUR SYSTEM! DETECTED MALICIOUS USER
CAN DAMAGE YOUR MACHINE AND COMPROMISE YOUR
PRIVACY. IT IS STRONGLY RECOMMENDED TO REMOVE
THEM IMMEDIATELY.

⟨ MESSAGE SENT ⟩

NICE TRY BREACHING MY SYSTEM. BUT I
CALCULATED IN ADVANCE YOUR FAILED ATTEMPT,
AND HAVE VIRUS SAFEGUARDS INSTALLED TO
PREVENT IT. I AM NOT THE MYSTERY EYE YOU ARE
LOOKING FOR, VIC_STONE. —NOAH

CLARK'S JOURNAL

As the search to find out who the Mystery Eye is continues, I've been pulled in two different directions, between my friends in the Justice Squad and helping Lois investigate at the school newspaper. And Bruce isn't happy in either case. I think he's mad we haven't been able to solve the mystery. But he's also mad at me for spending time away from the group. He seems grumpier than he's been. But maybe it's because he got caught by the principal breaking into school lockers to look for evidence. I never thought he could ever get caught, but even he slipped up and was seen by the principal.

Lately everything isn't adding up. First it was all the labs in school getting damaged and shut down through various accidents. Then Arthur was accused and suspended for it. We've also been unsuccessful finding any new leads. Vic tried to hack into Noah's special calculator, thinking he might be responsible, but Noah was ten steps ahead of us and knew he'd be a target and stopped us from finding out anything. Then Diana used her Lasso of Truth to interrogate other students. Even without the ability to lie, they still didn't say anything useful. And the notes Barry managed to swipe out of class were pretty meaningless.

I just found out the school photocopy machine has been damaged. I don't know if this is an act of sabotage or just anger for what's been going on. But now we can't even print up the school newspapers until it gets fixed. It's like everything is working against us, and we're no closer to figuring out who is behind it all!

ACCESS PORT = BATCAVE | ROOM = PRIVATE | USERS = ACTIVE (2) ☒

BAT = WITH ALL THE TROUBLE WE'VE HAD WITH MYSTERIOUS TEXTS

BAT = I THOUGHT IT MIGHT BE SAFER TO TALK TO YOU HERE

BAT = WHERE NO ONE CAN DROP IN

SUP = HOW CAN YOU BE SURE?

BAT = IT'S ME

BAT = I HAVE A STATE OF THE ART COMPUTER

BAT = AND THE BEST FIREWALLS TO PREVENT SPYING

SUP = OKAY

SUP = I HEAR YOU GOT CAUGHT RECENTLY

BAT = YEAH ABOUT THAT . . .

BAT = I GUESS I WASN'T PAYING ATTENTION

SUP = THAT'S NOT LIKE YOU

BAT = THANKS TO ME WE'RE NOW BEING WATCHED BY THE PRINCIPAL

BAT = HE WASN'T HAPPY

BAT = GAVE ME A WARNING

BAT = ACTUALLY ALL OF US A WARNING

BAT = BUT IT'S GIVEN ME AN IDEA

SUP = I'M NOT GOING TO LIKE THIS AM I?

BAT = I WANT YOU TO SNEAK INTO THE PRINCIPAL'S OFFICE

SEND

WRITE A MESSAGE

SUP = BRUCE I CAN'T!

BAT = JUST HEAR ME OUT

BAT = THERE'S GOT TO BE LOTS OF STUDENT AND TEACHER FILES IN THERE

BAT = PROBABLY LOCKED IN HIS DESK OR FILING CABINET

BAT = IT CAN BE USEFUL IN TRYING TO NARROW DOWN OUR SUSPECTS

SUP = I DON'T KNOW IF THIS IS A GOOD IDEA

SUP = ESPECIALLY AFTER HE JUST CAUGHT YOU AND OUR WARNING

BAT = LOOK . . . YOU'RE EXTREMELY FAST

BAT = PROBABLY AS FAST AS BARRY

SUP = THAT'S TRUE :)

BAT = YOU CAN BE IN AND OUT OF THERE BEFORE ANYONE WOULD NOTICE

BAT = BESIDES

BAT = WHAT WOULD LOIS WANT YOU TO DO

SUP = FIND OUT THE TRUTH

SUP = OKAY I'LL TRY

SEND

WRITE A MESSAGE

JUSTICE PREP

JUSTICE PREPARATORY ACADEMY
STUDENT STUDY GROUP & RELEASE FORM

The school district requires written authorization to administer its selected students into an involuntary private after-school program. By signing this release form, you give the school district authorization to place **CLARK KENT** into a disciplinary after-school studies program.

Ms. Amanda Waller, and the school district, shall not be held accountable for anything that happens during the course of this specialized study group and its educational pursuits.

As Justice Preparatory Academy is fully committed to the safety of all students, please complete this form and return to the school truancy officer and detention supervisor.

Student Name: Clark Kent

Truancy Officer/Detention Supervisor:
          Ms. Amanda Waller

Principal: James W. Gordon

120

TO: Principal_Gordon
FROM: The_Wall
SUBJECT: Detention Report

James,

I wanted to give you a quick update. The
exercise wasn't quite the success we wanted.
We hoped to give bad students a chance to
learn from their mistakes and not to repeat
them. They were offered that chance, but only
one of them changed.

Johnny Corben led the other students to break
into your office and take the green rock
placed there. A routine check on Johnny's
locker will most assuredly find he's hid
it there. As a result, I recommend his
disqualification from the school science fair
competition. And while the other students
went along with him, they don't deserve his
same fate. Leave them to me in detention and
I will work toward a better solution.

Clark Kent, on the other hand, refused to
take part. He seems like a good kid. Stood
his ground and didn't want to repeat what got
him in trouble in the first place. As far as
I'm concerned, he's served his time.

Before I sign off, there's one other student
I'd like to talk with you about transferring.
I've placed a letter in your office mailbox.

—Amanda

LOCUS
INSTITUTE OF HIGHER LEARNING

ATTN: Professor Ivo

Although student Winslow Schott has only a [   ]
short time, he has already made a positive an[   ]
am sad to see him go, but I am pleased to reco[   ]
institute that can make a difference in his life.

Winslow Schott appears to have cheated on a recent aptitude test. His high IQ score is suspicious following the recent trouble with the school's computer system being shut down. But I can't prove it. I just think this might become a black eye for the school if he enters the science fair, wins, and this is discovered upon further examination. I suggest we transfer him to a special gateway school for higher learning.

— Amanda

With his recent test scores placing him high on the academic spectrum, I believe he will be a great addition to your school. Winslow has proven himself to be highly motivated, creative, and extremely intelligent.

He's been a joy to teach and a fine student during his time here. And I know he'll make a great addition to your institution.

Sincerely,

James W. Gordon

James W. Gordon
Principal, Justice Preparatory Academy

THE JUSTICE TRIBUNE

SCI-FI GOOD-BYE
DISQUALIFICATIONS AND TRANSFERS PLAGUE CURRENT SCIENCE FAIR

BY LOIS LANE

No one can say that the lead-up to this year's science fair for Justice Prep has been boring.

We've already had one accused student dismissed from the competition in Arthur Curry, many classrooms vandalized and destroyed in the process, amid mysterious texting that's haunted the competition.

Add two more names to the list of casualties.

Johnny Corben, former reporter for this very newspaper, was disqualified from the competition when he was discovered with stolen property. A routine locker check located an item believed to have been taken from the office of our principal. When asked to comment, Principal James Gordon had very little to say. "I can't really go into detail. But disciplinary actions were taken on a student that was involved with theft."

Winslow Schott, on the other hand, has quickly left our school, seemingly of his own accord. A once promising student with a high GPA, he has moved to an undisclosed new school. His transfer was so sudden, he was unable to even clean out his locker. "It was filled with toys . . . lots and lots of toys," said one student who wished to go unnamed.

With a few weeks to go before the science fair ceremony takes place, anything can happen. And we'll report more about it right here!

I know you squealed on me, Kent. You knew all about that rock and told them to search my locker. You set me up, punk! I never trusted you and your goody-two-shoes attitude. You're so fake and fooling no one. Let's hash this out after school. You vs. me! I'm gonna make you pay!

JOHNNY

127

128

November 26th

CLARK'S JOURNAL

Almost got into a fight at school today over something stupid. Ma and Pa always told me not to fight with my fists, if my words could be a peaceful solution. But what happens when words won't fix things? I guess it helps having the ability to fly out of the way. I'm just glad Johnny didn't see me hovering up near the ceiling.

But that janitor saw me! No matter how many times I try to hide my powers, I always seem to get caught. I don't think he'll be a problem. He was actually pretty nice. Let me know he'd be around if I ever needed his help. He even offered me a cookie afterward, but I couldn't take it. I'd hate to upset Ma if I ruined my appetite before supper.

I still don't know what I want to do for my science fair experiment. But maybe going home will provide an answer.

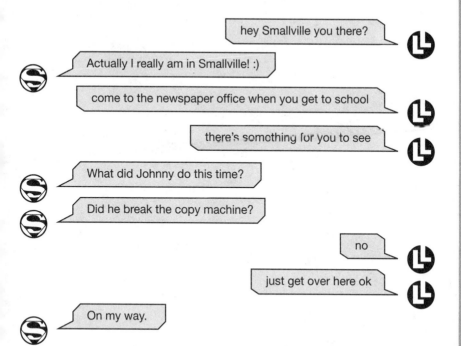

hey Smallville you there?

Actually I really am in Smallville! :)

come to the newspaper office when you get to school

there's something for you to see

What did Johnny do this time?

Did he break the copy machine?

no

just get over here ok

On my way.

SEND

Barry

Diana

TO CLARK KENT
c/o JUSTICE TRIBUNE

THOUGHT YOU'D BE INTERESTED
IN WHAT YOUR "FRIEND" HAS BEEN
UP TO.

—A CONCERNED STUDENT

BRUCE WAYNE / INVESTIGATION REPORT

NAME: CLARK KENT
SUSPECT: *HIGHLY LIKELY*

NOTES:

EVEN THOUGH HE'S MY FRIEND, IT DOESN'T RULE HIM OUT AS A SUSPECT. WHO BETTER
TO BE THE MYSTERY EYE THAN SOMEONE CLOSE TO ME. HE COULD EASILY BE LISTENING
TO ALL OF US, AND KNOWING IN ADVANCE WHAT WE'RE DOING TRYING TO FIND HIM. HE
MIGHT'VE FOUND A WAY TO TEXT US THOSE MESSAGES WITHOUT US KNOWING. AND HE'S
FAST ENOUGH TO BE IN TWO PLACES AT ONCE, CAUSING DAMAGE AND GETTING AWAY
BEFORE BEING CAUGHT. OUT OF EVERYONE, HE'S THE MOST LIKELY PERSON WHO COULD
DO ALL OF THIS.

I MIGHT HAVE TO PLACE A HIDDEN TRACKER ON HIM TO FOLLOW HIS MOVEMENTS. OR
SECRETLY BUG HIS PHONE. OR EVEN DESTROY HIS SCIENCE FAIR PROJECT SO HE CAN'T
WIN, SINCE I DON'T KNOW WHAT HIS END-GAME IS AT THIS POINT. IT WOULDN'T HURT
TO DO ALL THREE, JUST TO BE ON THE SAFE SIDE.

GROUP CHAT

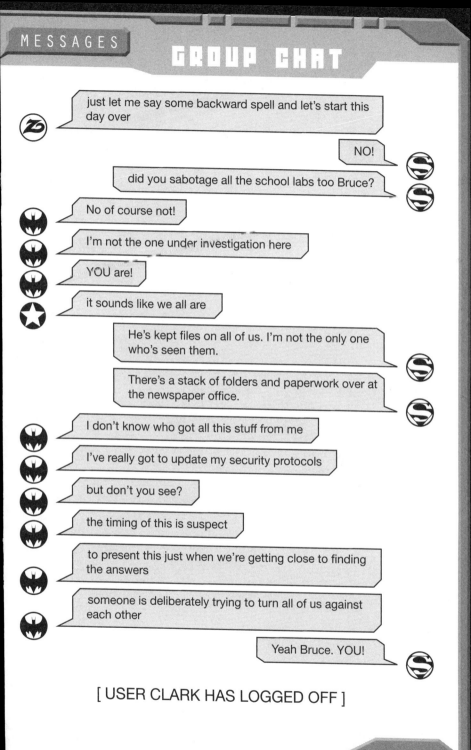

just let me say some backward spell and let's start this day over

NO!

did you sabotage all the school labs too Bruce?

No of course not!

I'm not the one under investigation here

YOU are!

it sounds like we all are

He's kept files on all of us. I'm not the only one who's seen them.

There's a stack of folders and paperwork over at the newspaper office.

I don't know who got all this stuff from me

I've really got to update my security protocols

but don't you see?

the timing of this is suspect

to present this just when we're getting close to finding the answers

someone is deliberately trying to turn all of us against each other

Yeah Bruce. YOU!

[USER CLARK HAS LOGGED OFF]

SEND

TO: BRUCE_WAYNE
CC: DIANA_PRINCE, BARRY_ALLEN, VIC_STONE,
ARTHUR_CURRY, OLIVER_QUEEN, ZATANNA_ZATARA
FROM: CLARK_KENT
SUBJECT: I QUIT!

I'M HEREBY RESIGNING FROM THE JUSTICE SQUAD.
I CAN'T BE A PART OF SOMETHING WHERE I'M
BEING ACCUSED OF A CRIME I DIDN'T COMMIT.
THAT MY OWN FRIEND IS THE ONE ACCUSING ME AND
EVEN SETTING ME UP TO FAIL IS WRONG. THAT ALL
OUR HARD WORK ON OUR SCIENCE FAIR PROJECTS
WOULD BE DESTROYED IS VERY CRUEL.

I WISH YOU LUCK IN FINDING WHO THE MYSTERY
EYE IS. IN THE END, I HOPE IT'S WORTH IT.

JUSTICE PREP

JUSTICE PREPARATORY ACADEMY
STUDENT INCIDENT REPORT

STUDENT: Barry Allen
TEACHER: Professor Eobard Thawne
CLASS: Science

DESCRIPTION OF INCIDENT: Barry was my only student missing from class. When I went out looking for him, I found him cutting my class. After a long chase, I was finally able to apprehend him. I would've brought him back to class to serve his time with me, except I was advised by the principal to escort him to the office.

ACTION TAKEN: Barry has been assigned after-school detention with Ms. Waller. He is to report to her classroom for further disciplinary action.

NOTES: Barry is to report to Room 10 immediately after school.

IF YOU HAVE ANY QUESTIONS ABOUT THIS EVENT, PLEASE CALL THE PRINCIPAL'S OFFICE

GEORGE HARKNESS
(aka Captain Boomerang)

LEONARD SNART
(aka Captain Cold)

HARTLEY RATHAWAY
(aka Pied Piper)

SAM SCUDDER
(aka Mirror Master)

JUSTICE PREP STUDENT BAKE SALE

Please join us for our bake sale fund-raiser. Due to various school lab closures, all monies raised go to support our student scientists to help them complete their projects for the upcoming science fair competition. We will have cupcakes, cakes, cookies, and other tasty treats available. Thank you for your support!

12 noon & 3 p.m.
Located in the Academy Auditorium

December 3rd

CLARK'S JOURNAL

Seeing everyone come together at the bake sale has given me second thoughts. Maybe I might've overreacted by quitting the Justice Squad. It's just that everyone is on edge not knowing who is trying to sabotage the science fair. And then my own friend, Bruce, trying to build a case against all of us being suspects was taking it too far. I understand being careful. But there's a difference between caution and letting paranoia get the best of us. And I let him get to me. I wish he didn't make me so mad sometimes, even if we don't always agree.

I heard that Barry's trip to detention has ruled out even more students as possible suspects. That's good. It sounds like those students weren't any sort of criminal masterminds. But this Mystery Eye still remains out there, on the eve of the science fair. I just hope nothing bad happens at the awards ceremony. But I'll be ready for it if it does.

YOU ARE CORDIALLY INVITED TO ATTEND:

THE 15TH ANNUAL
SCIENCE FAIR & AWARDS GALA

SUPPORTED **BY S.T.A.R. LABORATORIES,**
GENERAL DIRECTOR PROFESSOR EMIL HAMILTON,
DR. SAUL ERDEL, AND THE DISTRICT OF SCHOLARS

PRIZES AWARDED • OPEN HOUSE • FREE ADMISSION

12 NOON—DOORS OPEN

1:00 P.M.—OPENING CEREMONIES

2:00 P.M.—JUDGING BEGINS

3:00 P.M.—AWARDS PRESENTATION

REFRESHMENTS PROVIDED

THE STUDENTS HAVE BEEN WORKING ON THEIR PROJECTS
FOR THE PAST SCHOOL YEAR AND ARE EXCITED TO SHARE
THEM WITH THEIR FRIENDS, FAMILY, AND COMMUNITY.
COME TAKE PART IN ENCOURAGING THE NEXT
GENERATION OF SCIENTIFIC MINDS!

STUDENT: Clark Kent

PROJECT TITLE: Building a Rocket

PURPOSE: The universe is vast and infinite. To design a long-distance rocket that can travel outside our solar system, what is necessary to achieve the right trajectory? How far can it go before it stops?

STUDENT: Diana Prince

PROJECT TITLE: How to Make a Lie Detector

PURPOSE: Lying is a horrible trait. And not everyone has the ability to tie someone up to force them to tell the truth. But that's where a lie detector can be useful. I'm exploring how to make one and explore how body language and heart rate reveals if subjects are telling the truth.

STUDENT: Bruce Wayne

PROJECT TITLE: The Science of Fingerprints

PURPOSE: Exploring the science of forensics. Why do we have fingerprints? How are they used in crime scene investigations? The prints don't lie.

STUDENT: Barry Allen

PROJECT TITLE: Time Machine

PURPOSE: To create a time machine to travel anywhere. Or at the very least, run in place and get healthy. It also makes a cool ZOOM ZOOM sound, don't you think?

STUDENT: Vic Stone

PROJECT TITLE: The Future of Cybernetics

PURPOSE: How can technology help fix our bodies in the future? Will science be able to make us more machinelike? How can robotics help us function?

STUDENT: David Hyde

PROJECT TITLE: Hydropower

PURPOSE: The force of water is considered one of the strongest forces on the planet. How can it be harnessed? What can it be used for?

STUDENT: Joker Kid

PROJECT TITLE: Volcano-ho-ho

PURPOSE: Do cream pies taste better than fruit pies? Let's find out when my pie volcano erupts to create my pie-in-the-sky experiment. Hee hee hee.

STUDENT: Harleen Quinzel

PROJECT TITLE: Brain Gum

PURPOSE: Does chewing gum make you smarter? I don't know! Will somebody tell me?!

STUDENT: Pamela Isley

PROJECT TITLE: Effects of Acid Rain on Plant Growth

PURPOSE: To understand how acid rain affects plants over the short term and long term. Acid rain occurs when low-pH acids pollute our air and are deposited back on Earth when it rains, snows, sleets, or hails. Gases convert back to acids when they contact water. How can we help change the environment to stop this from occurring?

STUDENT: Noah Kuttler

PROJECT TITLE: Study Calculator Accuracy

PURPOSE: There have been a lot of changes and improvements since the very first calculator was invented. What are the different methods of testing calculators for their accuracy? And how can we create the ultimate calculator that won't be wrong?

<< WARNING >>

SUBJECT: DESPERO

ALIEN INVADER FROM DISTANT GALAXY. SELF-
PROFESSED CONQUEROR AND TYRANT. FAILED ATTEMPT
TO ACQUIRE S.T.A.R. LABS TECHNOLOGY TO HELP
OVERTAKE AND RULE THE GALAXY, LEADING TO
CAPTURE.

EXHIBITS A GENIUS INTELLECT AND ENHANCED MIND-
ALTERING POWERS WITH THIRD EYE ABILITY. ABLE
TO READ MINDS, CREATE ILLUSIONS, TELEKINESIS,
TELEPATHY, AND CAUSE HYPNOSIS. UNABLE TO
AFFECT ADULTS. HYPNOTIC TRANCE EFFECTS ARE
ABLE TO CONTROL LESS DEVELOPED CHILD MINDS
THROUGH TELEPATHIC LINK.

SCIENTIFIC DIAGNOSIS: UNABLE TO CLASSIFY
HIS MYSTICAL SOURCE OF PSIONIC POWER, WHICH
GRANTS HIM SUPERHUMAN STRENGTH, DURABILITY,
SPEED, AND THE ABILITY TO ALTER HIS BIOMASS
(TO REINTEGRATE HIMSELF IN SIZE, MOLECULE BY
MOLECULE).

ANALYSIS: EXTREMELY DANGEROUS! PROCEED WITH
CAUTION!

THE JUSTICE TRIBUNE

[D]ESPERATE TIMES CALL [F]OR DESPERO MEASURES

[B]Y CLARK KENT

One of S.T.A.R. Labs' greatest achievements almost became its greatest disaster. Scientist Dr. Saul Erdel is the man responsible for creating an experimental teleportation beam as a means to chart and study the galaxy. But once activated, it opened a doorway across the universe and accidentally transported two alien life-forms to the laboratory. One of them, called Despero, a self-proclaimed warrior and conqueror, hated being pulled here and turned violent until his capture. The other life-form, known as the Martian Manhunter, liked Earth and blended in with humans to work with us.

Despero nearly destroyed the science fair event held at S.T.A.R. Labs, but with the quick thinking of many students from neighboring Justice Preparatory Academy, Despero has been recaptured. The scientists at S.T.A.R. Labs will continue to work with Erdel and the Martian Manhunter to find a way to safely return each of them back to space. And the teleportation beam has been shut down, and is awaiting more analysis before it can be properly used again.

MY INTERVIEW WITH JEKYLL AND HYDE

BY LOIS LANE

"He's always been my adversary. But I never thought it would turn out this way."

Such are the words of student David Hyde, commenting on his relationship with Arthur Curry. Both students are two of the school's top swimmers, and have met in many swim meet competitions. But wanting an extra edge in defeating his opponent helped sway David to a dark offer.

"When this Mystery Eye first contacted me, I'd do it, if it helped me win the science fair and beat my rival," said David.

Only later was I able to convince it that I'd do it, if it only wanted a favor: for me to free it from its prison.

And by winning the science fair, it would allow David access into S.T.A.R. Labs in order to free his benefactor, an alien named Despero. But David still wrestles with his participation in this event.

"Was I under its hypnotic influence the whole time? Or did I do some of this willingly?" asks David.

"I'm afraid to find out. But what I'm not afraid of is saying that I'm sorry. And I hope I can make it up to Arthur. And make it up to everyone."

Let's hope he is given that chance.

TO: Clark_Kent
FROM: Lois_Lane
SUBJECT: Great job, Smallville!

It's not every day that I allow someone else to steal the front page headline. But I feel you earned it, farm boy. Great job finding out who the Mystery Eye was, and also finding out about Dr. Erdel and his teleportation beam. S.T.A.R. Labs is notoriously shy when it comes to revealing information about their technology and facility. But you somehow managed to get the scoop before anyone else (including me)!

So I guess, if you want, you can stick around at the paper. I'm not promising any further spots on the front page. But who knows. With enough hard work, maybe you'll make a good reporter someday.

—Lois

P.S. Let's do lunch at school. You're buying.

TO: Bruce_Wayne
CC: Diana_Prince, Barry_Allen, Vic_Stone, Arthur_Curry, Oliver_Queen, Zatanna_Zatara
FROM: Clark_Kent
SUBJECT: I'm sorry

I was wrong to get mad at you, Bruce. And to leave the Justice Squad. I realize now that we were all just trying to get to the truth. And fear affected each of us in different ways. It got the better of me and made me mad. But if Ma and Pa Kent ever taught me anything, it's to do right and realize when we're wrong. I'm sorry.

I hope you all can forgive me. And I hope you'll let me rejoin the group. I miss you all. And still think there's so much more good we can do together.

Thanks!

CLARK'S JOURNAL

In the end, everything turned out well. I've rejoined the Justice Squad! Before I was able to send my email out to everyone, Bruce approached me to apologize, which is a first. He took all the files he'd been keeping on every student and destroyed them. Even the files he kept on all his friends. Bruce never ceases to amaze me. He might seem like a grump at times, but he has a good heart and good intentions.

Arthur had his suspension lifted and is back in school with us. It's good to have him around again. And they awarded him first place in the science fair. As part of winning, he asked to have our whole school join him to visit the new space observatory. A very unselfish move. In a way, it felt like we all won!

But maybe the best thing to come out of all of this is realizing there appear to be other nice aliens out in the universe. I don't have to feel alone anymore. And if I'm ever in trouble, there's even more friends who will be there to help.

One day, I hope I can travel out to the stars and see the universe. It would be a great adventure. Even if Bruce isn't as excited about that idea. He says it would make him space sick.

Derek Fridolfs

Derek Fridolfs is a *New York Times* bestselling writer. With Dustin Nguyen, he co-wrote the Eisner-nominated *Batman: Li'l Gotham*. He's also worked on a range of titles including *Arkham City* with Paul Dini, *Adventures of Superman*, *Detective Comics*, *Sensation Comics Featuring Wonder Woman*, and *Biff to the Future* with producer/screenwriter Bob Gale. He's written and drawn comics based on the cartoons for *Adventure Time*, *Regular Show*, *Clarence*, *Pig Goat Banana Cricket*, *Pink Panther's The Inspector*, *Dexter's Laboratory*, *Teenage Mutant Ninja Turtles*, *Teen Titans Go!*, *Looney Tunes*, and *Scooby-Doo, Where Are You!* He's also written chapter books for Capstone based on the Justice League.

Pamela Lovas

Pamela Lovas started her career working in Marvel Comics' digital department, before moving on to freelance for a variety of comic companies, including DC, IDW, Boom Studios, and Dynamite Entertainment. She's drawn and colored for such properties as *Adventure Time*, *Regular Show*, *Scooby-Doo, Where Are You!*, *Looney Tunes*, *Teen Titans Go!*, *Back to the Future*, and Funko Pop Universe *X-Files*. This is her first time illustrating a children's book.

Shane Clester

Shane Clester has been a professional illustrator since 2005. Initially working in comics and storyboards, Shane has transitioned to his real passion—children's books. Shane currently lives in Florida with his wonderful wife and their two tots. When not illustrating, he can usually be found by his in-laws' pool.